Where is Mr. Kim?

VISTA
HIGHER LEARNING

Boston, Massachusetts

Luiz, Jakob, and Andrea are students, and they are also good friends. They are 18 years old, and they all go to Norwood High School. They like their school and all their teachers, but their favorite teacher is Mr. Kim.

Mr. Kim is a cool teacher. He gets along well with all of the students at the school. He's fun, interesting, and he has a great **sense of humor**!

look for

hide

Mr. Kim hides things. He puts them in new and different places.

Mr. Kim likes to **organize** interesting **activities** for his students. His most popular activity is the Mystery Game. Once a year, Mr. Kim hides different things around the school. Then, he writes **clues**. Students read the clues and look for the things. It's a great way for students to get better at reading. New students can also learn more about the school. Plus, everyone has a great time!

EXTRA!

What makes a good teacher? Students like teachers who are **good communicators** and who have lots of **energy**. They also like teachers who are helpful, nice, funny, and fair.

It's the day of Mr. Kim's Mystery Game. Luiz, Andrea, and Jakob are excited, so they go to his classroom. But where is Mr. Kim? Normally he's in the classroom or busy organizing things for the game. But this year, he's not around.

The friends decide to go to the main office and ask the **principal**, Ms. Saryan.

"Hi, Ms. Saryan," says Luiz. "It's time for Mr. Kim's Mystery Game, but we can't find him. Do you know where he is?"

"I'm sorry, I don't know where he is right now," answers Ms. Saryan. "I saw him this morning. Try looking in his office."

"OK. Thanks, Ms. Saryan," says Andrea. "We'll find him!"

MR. KIM'S OFFICE

jacket

phone

They knock on the door.
They softly hit the door.

The three friends go to Mr. Kim's office. It seems pretty quiet. Luiz knocks on the door and waits. "Hello?" Andrea says, looking around. "Mr. Kim? Are you there?"

No answer.

Andrea looks through the window. She sees Mr. Kim's desk. "Look," she says. "There's his jacket! And his phone! He can't be far away!"

KNOW IT ALL

More than 50 percent of people aged 18–34 carry their phones around all day.

"Hmm," says Jakob, looking around the hallway. "Where is he? He must be somewhere. . . ."

The friends see the **school counselor**, Ms. Klopp, coming down the hallway. "Excuse me, Ms. Klopp," Luiz calls. "Do you know where Mr. Kim is?"

Ms. Klopp stops to think. "I'm not sure," she says. "Maybe he's in the **cafeteria**. It's still lunchtime."

"Thank you!" the friends call as they hurry away.

MR. KIM'S OFFICE

cafeteria

custodian

CAUTION WET FLOOR

The friends go to the cafeteria. They see several students eating, drinking, and talking. Unfortunately, Mr. Kim is not there.

Then they see Mr. O'Brien, the **custodian**. He's cleaning the floor. He works all around the school, so Andrea decides to ask him about Mr. Kim.

"Excuse me, Mr. O'Brien," she says. "Do you know where Mr. Kim is?"

"Sorry, I don't know where he is right now," says Mr. O'Brien. "But I have an idea. I know Mr. Kim really likes sports. Maybe he's in the gym. He said that he had volleyball practice today."

"Great idea! Thanks, Mr. O'Brien," says Jakob. Then, he looks at his friends and says, "Come on. Let's look for Mr. Kim in the gym!"

volleyball practice

KNOW IT ALL

Volleyball was created by a man named William G. Morgan and was first played in 1895. It became an Olympic sport in 1964.

The Norwood High School gym is pretty big. In the middle, some kids are playing volleyball, but no one else is there. The friends look around. Is Mr. Kim here? No, he's not. So where is he?

The friends are running out of ideas—and time. They need about an hour to play the Mystery Game, and the school day is almost over!

Then, Jakob sees a volleyball player that he knows. "Hi Anna," he says. "We're looking for Mr. Kim. Have you seen him?"

"I'm sorry, I haven't," answers Anna. "He didn't come to volleyball practice today."

"OK, thanks," says Jakob.

KNOW IT ALL

Nearly eight million US students play high school sports. It's a great way to meet people and have fun!

"I don't understand," says Andrea. "Mr. Kim never misses volleyball practice. And now he misses the Mystery Game? This is very strange!"

"I know," says Luiz with a worried look on his face. "Mr. Kim loves helping with volleyball practice. I know he wouldn't miss it."

"Come on," says Jakob. "Let's ask Ms. Saryan again. Maybe Mr. Kim **is in trouble**."

"Hi there," says Ms. Saryan. "Was Mr. Kim in his office?"

"No," says Luiz. "He wasn't in his office, or in the cafeteria, or in the gym. We're worried, Ms. Saryan. Maybe Mr. Kim is in trouble!"

"Hmm. It is a bit strange," says Ms. Saryan. "Now I'm worried, too. Let's look in the art room. I saw him there this morning."

Ms. Saryan and the friends go to the art room. There are lots of pictures on the walls, but there is no Mr. Kim.

"He's not here," says Ms. Saryan. "Maybe we can . . . "

"Wait," says Luiz. "I hear something. It's coming from the closet."

They try the closet door, but it's **locked**. Ms. Saryan uses her key to open it and slowly looks in.

It's Mr. Kim! "Thank you so much for **saving** me!" he says, smiling. "I was hiding something for the Mystery Game, and the door locked behind me!"

"Are you OK?" asks Ms. Saryan.

"Yes," says Mr. Kim. "I'm fine. But I'm really sorry kids. There's no time for our Mystery Game now."

"Don't worry, Mr. Kim," explains Luiz. "We *had* a Mystery Game. This year's mystery was finding you!"

(good) sense of humor the ability to say, do, and understand funny things

organize to make plans for something

activity something people do for fun or enjoyment

clue a small piece of information that helps you find the answer to a game or problem

good communicator someone who is good at talking to people

energy the power to do a lot of things

principal the leader of a school

school counselor a person whose job is helping students

cafeteria the place at a school, office or other place where people buy and eat food

custodian a person who cleans and repairs things in a building

be in trouble to be in danger of having bad things happen

locked closed and needing a key to open

save to help someone or something get away from danger